GROUNDHUG DAY

written by ANNE MARIE PACE

illustrations by CHRISTOPHER DENISE

𝒟ISNℰ𝒴 • HYPERION

Los Angeles   New York

For my writer friends, especially WRT4KDZ-ers,
SCBWI-ers, and those who quack
—A.M.P.

For all my friends at Kindling Words,
who coax me out of the studio at least once a year
—C.D.

Valentine's Day was only two weeks away, and Moose was planning a grand party.

"You need Valentine balloons!"
said Squirrel.
"And Valentine cards!"
said Bunny.

"And don't forget the Valentine hugs!"
pointed out Porcupine.

"Everyone has to come to my party," said Moose.

"Uh-oh," Bunny said. "That's a problem."

"What's a problem?" Moose asked.

"Tomorrow is Groundhog Day," Bunny said.
"If Groundhog sees his shadow, he'll go back into
his hole for six more weeks. He won't be awake on
February 14th."

"Good point!" Moose said. "If we stop him from
seeing his shadow, then he can come to my party."

"I've got it!" said Squirrel. "I'll sneak into his hole and change his calendar so he won't know it's February 2nd."

"Your chattering will wake him up," said Porcupine.

"I'll blindfold him when he comes out."

"Your quills might poke him in the eye,"
said Bunny. "I'll put up a tent over his hole."

"He'll know he's not outside," Moose said.

"I'll sit on his hole so he can't come out at all."

"Calendar!"

"Moose!"

"Blindfold!"

"Moose!"

"Tent!"

"Moose!" bellowed Moose.

The animals bickered all night long.

They didn't notice the black sky turning gray.

They didn't notice the pink light of
morning creeping over the hills.
And they didn't notice Groundhog's nose
twitching at the entrance to his hole—

until

it

was

too

late.

The animals watched helplessly as
Groundhog dove back into his hole.
"WAIT!" Moose thundered.

Groundhog's muffled voice
barely reached the surface.
"I need to stay down here. There are
shadows all over the place up there."

Moose was puzzled.

"Groundhog? Are you afraid?

Is that why you go back into your hole?"

"You could say that," Groundhog called.

"I didn't realize Groundhog was afraid
of shadows," said Squirrel.

"Me neither," said Porcupine.

"Shadows aren't scary," said Bunny.

"They are scary to Groundhog," Moose said.

The animals sat quietly, thinking.

"Hey, Groundhog," Moose finally said. "What if we showed you just how awesome shadows are? I'll show you the ways leaves blowing in the wind make shadows that dance!"

"I'll show you how to draw silhouettes!" said Bunny.

"I'll show you how clouds cast shadows on the hills," said Squirrel.

"I want to show Groundhog my shadow puppets!"
said Porcupine.

"Dancing shadows!"
Moose said.

"Cloud shadows!"
Squirrel said.

"Silhouettes!"
Bunny said.

"Shadow puppets!"
said Porcupine.

"WAIT!"

said Groundhog.

He eased out of his hole.

"Can't we do ALL of them?

They ALL sound fun."

The animals spent the day showing
Groundhog all the amazing shadows
they could discover and create.

And they WERE all fun, especially
Porcupine's shadow puppets.

Finally, late that night . . .

"What a wonderful day!" Groundhog said.

"But I really do have to go back into my hole now."

He shivered.

"Six more weeks of winter, you know."

"But you're not afraid of shadows anymore," Moose protested. "Now you don't have to miss my Valentine's Day party."

"I may not be *afraid*,"
Groundhog said,
"but it is *cold* up here."

"But there aren't any balloons in your hole," said Squirrel.

"Or Valentine cards!" said Bunny.

"Or Valentine hugs!" said Porcupine pointedly.

"Nope. But my hole is *warm*," said Groundhog.
He looked at his disappointed friends.
"We can at least have hugs before I go.
Groundhugs all around—with a special
Groundhog Day Nose-Kiss for you, Porcupine."
"That works for me! Happy Groundhug Day!"
said Porcupine.

Six weeks later,

Groundhog emerged from his den just in time
to don a green hat.

"Let's have a St. Patrick's Day party!" he hollered.
"We're all here!"

"All but Bunny," Squirrel reminded Groundhog.

"Where's Bunny?" Groundhog asked.

"Oh, you know Bunny," Moose said.

"He's always holed up this time of year."

First Edition, December 2017
10 9 8 7 6 5 4 3 2 1
FAC-029191-17293
Printed in Malaysia

This book is set in Adobe Caslon Pro, Chorxy/Fontspring
Designed by Phil Caminiti
Illustrations created digitally using Photoshop and a Wacom tablet

Library of Congress Cataloging-in-Publication Data

Names: Pace, Anne Marie, author. • Denise, Christopher, illustrator.
Title: Groundhug Day / by Anne Marie Pace ; illustrated by Christopher Denise.
Description: First edition. • Los Angeles ; New York : Disney-Hyperion, 2017.
Summary: "Moose is planning the biggest Valentine's Day party ever. But
can he convince his friend, Groundhog, to stay around to celebrate without
hiding from his shadow?"—Provided by publisher.
Identifiers: LCCN 2016054232 • ISBN 9781484753569 (hardcover)
ISBN 1484753569 (hardcover)
Subjects: CYAC: Moose—Fiction. • Woodchuck—Fiction. • Forest
Animals—Fiction. • Shadows—Fiction. • Valentine's Day—Fiction.
Classification: LCC PZ7.P113 Gro 2017 • DDC [E]—dc23
LC record available at https://lccn.loc.gov/2016054232

Reinforced binding
Visit www.DisneyBooks.com